Jump and Fly

Written and illustrated by Petr Horáček

The bird.

The bird tweets.

The bird jumps.

The bird falls!

The bird flaps.

The bird flies!

Jump and fly

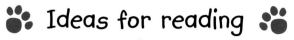 Ideas for reading

Written by Clare Dowdall, PhD
Lecturer and Primary Literacy Consultant

Learning objectives: children read and understand simple sentences; they answer 'how' and 'why' questions about their experiences and in response to stories and events; children talk about how they and others show feelings

Curriculum links: Understanding of the world: The world

High frequency words: the

Interest words: jump, fly, bird, flies, tweets, falls, flaps

Resources: whiteboard, card, split pins, scissors, pencils, feathers

Word count: 17

Getting started

- Tell children about a bird's nest that you have seen, and describe it to them. Ask children to suggest why birds have nests, and what sometimes happens in a nest. Explain that this book is about a chick in a nest.

- Look at the front cover together. Read the title and ask children to describe what they can see and predict what is going to happen to the bird in this story.

Reading and responding

- Turn to p2 and read the text. Help children to read the words by using the clues in the picture and by sounding out the phonemes.

- Ask children to describe what they can see on p2 and support them to use adventurous vocabulary. Help them to connect this to the illustration on p3, e.g. the bird's nest is high up in the tree.

- Ask children to read to the end of the story to find out what happens to the bird. Listen as they read and support them to sound out longer words and to reread sentences fluently.